super power kids

GW00993543

m2f

Published by
m2f publishing limited
5 Windlesham Avenue
Brighton BN1 3AH
England.

Text © **m2f** publishing limited 2004
Illustrations © Fred Pipes 2004
All rights reserved

The moral right of the illustrator has been asserted

Made and printed in the UK.

Except in the United States of America, this book is
sold subject to the condition that it shall not, by way
of trade or otherwise, be lent, re-sold, hired out, or
otherwise circulated without the publisher's prior
consent in any form of binding or cover other than
that in which it is published and without a similar
condition including this condition being imposed on
the subsequent purchaser.

British Library Cataloguing in Publication Data
A CIP catalogue record for this book is available
from the British Library

ISBN: 1-904948-01-4

super power kids

written by
Anthony Bullock

illustrated by
Fred Pipes

monday 2 friday books
one story five bedtimes

m2f publishing limited

contents

Specially written for grown-ups to read
to children aged 5-8, **m2f** books help
with the bedtime routine. Each chapter
is the same length – around 10-15 minutes
reading out loud – full of fun and
adventure for you and your children to
enjoy together. Now everyone will look
forward to bedtime.

It didn't look like an ordinary sweet – there was something special about it. It certainly wasn't one that Ella had ever seen before. And when you get to nine, well nearly ten years old, you've seen a lot of sweets.

Ella looked for her mum. She was over at the coffee shed gossiping to Ben's mum and being all gooey-eyed over Ben's little brother Archie. She looked round for Ben. He was hanging out on the big slide.

Ella and Ben had grown up together. Their mums had been friends even before they were born. When they were younger, people thought they were brother and sister – perhaps because they both had green

eyes and light wavy hair. Now Ella had
let her blond hair grow long and tangly.
Ben's hair had turned browner and he wore
it shaved at the sides and short on top. No
one mistook them for brother and sister any
more and they didn't play together so much
either. But the sweet was his kind of thing.

"Ben," she called, ambling across to the
bottom of the slide.

He glanced down, careful not to look
too interested.

"Come and look at this," she shouted up,
waving her hand.

"What?"

"Come on," she said, nodding over her
shoulder, not wanting to reveal her treasure
to the whole park.

He didn't come straight away. She could
tell he was checking out whether there
might be a better offer; whether anyone
would see him go down the slide; whether
that would be cool.

'I'll do it on my own,' she thought. She turned back towards the bench. She could still see the sweet sparkling in the sunlight. No one else was near it. The skateboarders on the ramp nearby were just doing their thing. A dog wandered by and didn't even stop to sniff.

Ella sat on the bench next to the sweet as the dog's owner shuffled past. She allowed her hand to close around the wrapper with one last guilty glance towards her mum. She knew you shouldn't eat sweets you find. But this one had a wrapper. And it wasn't being offered by a stranger. She wouldn't go near a sweet offered by a stranger.

"What is it?"

Ben's voice startled her. She hadn't seen him follow her. She let her fingers unfurl and saw his face open up.

"Where did you get that?" he asked, all excited, cool forgotten.

"I found it here."

He took it from her. It looked like silver foil, but felt like a summer dress your granny wears. It twinkled as if covered in a shimmering dust, but was entirely smooth.

"Shall I open it?" Ben asked.

One last guilty glance at her mum. Ella nodded.

The wrapper unwound without making a sound, revealing a bright green, glazed shiny sweet about three centimetres long.

Ben laughed a little nervously.

"Half each?" he asked.

Ella suddenly felt she should say 'no', but it was too late. Ben bit into it halfway along before she could stop him. A soft, orange, stringy gloop dribbled from his bottom lip as he tried to pull it apart. He handed half the sweet to her, smiling and nodding enthusiastically.

Ella had the strange feeling someone was watching. Ah, but she was always too cautious.

Why not? She popped it in her mouth.

Ben started to laugh.

Where she'd expected a fizzy sherbet taste, she got something smooth and dull. It wasn't horrible – you wouldn't spit it out – but it didn't taste sparkly or even green.

'Mashed potato,' she thought.

Ben hopped up and down nodding, with a finger on his nose.

"You've got it," he said, when his mouth was clear. "Mashed potato. Or something like that. Weird."

Ella stopped chewing. She still had a mouthful. Surely she hadn't said "mashed potato" out loud? She'd only thought it!

"You must have said it out loud," Ben said as he scanned the park, "or else how could I have heard you?"

Ella grabbed his shoulders and turned Ben to face her.

'Watch my lips,' she thought.

Ben jumped back. "But I can hear you saying it."

'Saying what?' she thought.

"You've done it again!"

'You try,' she thought at him.

He looked back blankly.

"Try and think something and see if I can read your mind," she said out loud.

He looked back, blankly again.

'Come on you idiot,' she thought, 'it's not that difficult to think things is it?'

"Don't call me an idiot," he said. "I was doing it. You're the idiot! You obviously can't read my mind, but I can read yours!"

How had it happened? Why was it happening? Was it the mashed potato sweet? If it was, why hadn't it affected her?

 "Will you stop blathering your thoughts all over the place?"

Ben said crossly, "I can't think with you thinking in my head."

'I can't not think,' she thought huffily to herself.

"Well go and do it somewhere else," he said, kicking out at the bench with the side of his foot.

Ella couldn't believe what she saw next: His foot rebounded with such a force that it knocked his other foot away and he landed in a heap on the ground.

"What happened there?" Ella asked.

Ben looked shocked as he got to his feet. He slumped against a tree, but he seemed to bounce off it as if it were rubber.

"What is it?" Ella asked.

Ben turned to the tree and gave it kick. Nothing. Then he turned sideways on and jumped at it with

his shoulder. This time he pinged off the trunk like it was a rope from a wrestling ring. "Cool," he said. "I've got some kind of superpower!"

"Ella!" It was her mum. "We've got to go and get your sisters. Say goodbye to Ben."

"You can't go now!" he said.

"Can I come back with Ben, mum?"

"No, sorry. We've got to go on to Daisy's for tea, remember? Come on love. Ooh, look at that pretty wrapper!"

Ella picked it up and put it in her pocket. Then she started thinking.

'I'm going to keep thinking all the way to Daisy's. You can tell me at school if you could hear me all the way. And Ben, whatever you do, be careful with the bouncing thing. You could really get in trouble with it. Right, we're going through the gates and up Brisbane terrace…'

Ella's mum had a go at her for sulking, but she was determined to keep sending Ben messages all the way there. When they got to Daisy's, both of Ella's little sisters were in the garden, playing off-ground 'he' with Daisy.

It was a really big garden with loads of old trees, and logs lying around the edges of a lawn – plenty of places to get off the ground. The game was in full swing; Ella's five-year-old sister, Ruby, was 'it'. Ella ran past her and scrambled onto an old tree stump. When Ruby passed, Ella jumped back down, landing on both feet. But instead of standing on the grass she found herself bouncing upwards at such a speed

she had to grab a branch
to stop herself from
disappearing up into the tree.

"Hey, that's not fair!"
Ruby squealed.

Ella felt a bit dazed. Did she
have new powers too?

"You're not allowed to climb
trees, Ella. That's too high,"
Ruby shouted at her, stamping
her foot.

"Hey look – Daisy's over there,"
Ella called back and watched Ruby
run off again.

Ella gingerly climbed down the tree,
legs shaking a little. When she got to the
bottom, she checked that no one was
looking and tried a hop. Nothing.
She must have imagined it. She took a
deep breath and did a tiny two-footed jump
– leaving the squishy lawn by no more than
a few centimetres.

Whoosh. The second she landed on the grass, she shot up to knee height off the ground. The next time she landed, she was sent soaring again, this time over waist height – perhaps even head height. Rather than land on her feet, she folded them up behind her and half landed on her knees and hands. It hurt a little, but it stopped her, which was all that mattered.

Ruby came running over. "I'm going to get you now!"

"Ruby, I'm sorry. I've twisted my ankle. I'll have to stop for a while."

What was she going to do? How could she explain it all without admitting she'd eaten a strange sweet in the park – something she knew she wasn't allowed to do?

All Ella wanted was to sit down quietly
somewhere and think, but her middle sister
Charlotte went and got her mum and Ella
had to limp heavily inside.

"Does this hurt?" her mother asked, gently
moving her ankle from one side to another
and bending her foot. Daisy's mum brought
her a glass of water and Ruby was running
around saying it wasn't her fault and Ella
shouldn't have been climbing trees anyway.

Ella winced and drank the water and
nodded at the worried grown-ups. She kept
the shoe off until it was time to go home so
that she could remember which foot to limp
on. When they got back to the flat, she
went straight to bed, just saying that she
thought her ankle needed
rest and that she
was sure it
would be
fine in the
morning.

And that's what she hoped for most. That she would wake up in the morning and she would be normal again. No special powers; no one reading her thoughts; just a normal Tuesday with boring lessons, ordinary lunch and no sweets.

That's it for tonight

Sleep well. We'll find out more about Ella and Ben and their superpowers next time, in superpower kids.

tuesday

m2f

What happened last time?

*Ella found a sweet in the park. It had a strange sparkly
wrapper like no other sweet she had ever seen before
(and at the age of nearly ten, she'd seen a lot of sweets
in her time). She got her friend Ben over to have a look.
Even though they both knew they shouldn't touch it,
they ate half each. They were just getting over the
disappointment that the sweet actually tasted of mashed
potato rather than sherbet when Ella discovered that Ben
could hear her thoughts as clearly as if she were speaking
out loud. Then he kicked the bench and they found that his
legs were like rubber, shooting all over the place. Then Ella
discovered that she too had a new special power – if she
jumped with both feet she shot upwards like someone on a
supercharged bouncy castle. Ella was scared by these new
powers and went to bed hoping that when she woke up,
everything would be back to normal. Now read on...*

Ella woke up to find her dad sitting
on the side of her bed.

"Mum says you hurt your ankle at
Daisy's last night. Which one was it?"

Ella thought hard.

"This one," she said offering
her right one.

She watched as her
dad went through

pretty much the same routine
her mum had done the
afternoon before, bending
her foot from side to side,
up and down.

"I can't see any swelling," he said,
stroking her hair out of her eyes. "Are you
sure that's why you went to bed early?"

She'd actually quite like to tell him what
it was really about but she didn't know if
she still had the power (or the problem, as
she thought of it). There wasn't much point
in blurting it all out if it wasn't still there.
He probably wouldn't even believe her.

"It's fine. Let me try walking on it,"
she said, sliding out of bed and putting
her weight on both feet.

Did they feel springy? Difficult to tell.
She got up and walked a few paces.

"It feels OK, dad, thanks."

"Right then, you'd better get a move on.
It's quarter-past eight already."

Ella walked into the bathroom ready to try a little hop, but Ruby and Charlotte were both in there cleaning their teeth.

When Ella had got her school clothes on, she ducked into her sisters' room and eyed the bunk beds. She could just do a jump in here and grab the top bunk to stop it getting out of hand. It all seemed a bit mad. Had it really happened? She bent her knees. Not too hard.

"What are you doing?" her mum's voice

squawked, head peering round the door.

"Looking for my sweater," Ella said quickly, feet still firmly on the ground.

"You're wearing it, you daft girl. I don't know what's got into you. You're going to be late. Dad's going to give you all a lift but you've still got hair, breakfast, teeth and shoes to do, so come on."

Ella wasn't left alone for a moment; when they got to school the whistle had already gone, so she didn't get a chance to test her jumping powers. Nor did she see Ben.

As Mr James took them through chunking down in maths problems yet again, Ella tried banging her feet gently on the floor under her chair. She still couldn't really tell. She half stood and was about to try a tiny jump when she had the awful feeling that everyone was looking at her.

They were.

"Boring you, am I, Ella Bryant?"

"No sir, sorry sir. I just need to go to the

toilet, sir," she blurted out, trying to ignore the giggles around her.

"Well perhaps you could put your hand up like normal people do?"

Could he tell she wasn't normal? "Yes sir. Sorry sir."

She ran to the toilets and was pleased to find that she was alone. Shutting a cubicle door, she held on to the toilet roll holder with one hand and tried a tentative hop. Nothing happened. At least nothing out of the ordinary. Her heart did a little skip – perhaps she'd imagined it all? Dreamt it even? Holding on to the toilet roll with both hands she now tried a tiny jump with both feet.

Wham! The toilet roll came off in her hand and she pinged upwards. The only thing she could think of was to land on the toilet seat to stop from bouncing again.

It broke noisily and she ended up with her
bottom jammed in the toilet, the broken
toilet roll holder still in her hand.

Ella stayed absolutely
still, waiting to hear
if anyone was
coming. When
she was sure no
one had heard,
she pushed herself
out of the toilet. Putting
the broken bits in a pile in the corner of the
cubicle, she shot out of the toilets – straight
into the headmistress.

"Did you hear a noise, Ella?"
Mrs Lopez asked.

"Er, no miss. No, I didn't."

"Right. Well back to class with you,"
she said.

Ella nodded, and began walking back
along the corridor.

"Ella?" Mrs Lopez called. "How did your

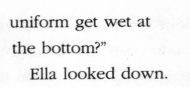

uniform get wet at the bottom?"

Ella looked down. Her blue school skirt was black along the bottom where it had soaked up the water from the toilet.

"Er, I just washed something off it," Ella said, continuing to walk.

When she got back to class, Mr James was in full flow at the blackboard.

Ella tried to squeeze behind her desk quietly without drawing attention to herself, but without even turning his head he immediately asked her a question.

"How did you do with these in your homework, Ella?"

She could feel herself going red.
"I hurt my ankle last night, so I went
straight to bed."

"But you've got a note? Or a bandage?
Or both?"

"No. Sorry sir. I woke up late."

"I'll tell you what Ella, rather than bore
the class with your tall tales, you can stay
behind at the end and talk to me, OK?"

"Yes sir."

Great. Now she wouldn't get to see
Ben at break time either. Then she heard
the classroom door open. She couldn't
bear to look.

"Sorry to disturb you Mr James, but I was
just wondering if it might be possible to see
Ella Bryant after class?"

Ella blushed again as she turned to face
Mrs Lopez who was standing in the
doorway with bits of broken toilet seat
in one hand and an unattached toilet roll
holder in the other.

"Take her now if you like.
She's not making much of
a contribution here."

"No. After class will
be fine thank you,
Mr James." With that,
she shut the door.

Ella was scarlet
now. And panicking.
What was she going to
say to Mrs Lopez? At least
she had twenty minutes to
think of something.

When the bell went, she made her way to
Mrs Lopez's office. The toilet seat was on
her desk.

"Well, young lady?"

"Um, I stood on the toilet roll holder and
it broke and I fell off onto the toilet seat."

"And would it be rude to ask why you
stood on the toilet roll holder? Do you have

a different way of using toilets from the rest of us?"

Ella knew that the next bit was a bit weak, but it was the best she'd been able to come up with.

"No miss. I just wanted to see if the ceiling moved."

"I beg your pardon?"

"My dad's a builder and he was talking about hanging ceilings. I just wondered if that was one..." She trailed off.

"And will he be happy to pay for the damage you've done, do you think?"

"I don't know, miss." Ella felt like crying. She never got into trouble. This shouldn't be happening.

"This is not like you Ella. Is there something else?"

Ella panicked. Could Mrs Lopez read her mind too? 'You're as mad as a fish, Mrs Lopez,' she thought to herself.

"Ella? Is there something else you want to tell me?"

'Yes, I ate a sweet and now I've got superpowers,' she thought to herself.

"No miss," she said out loud.

"Right. Well drop by the office at the end of school and pick up a letter for your father. Now get out of my sight before I think of some serious punishment."

"Yes miss. Thanks, miss."

Ella had to see Mr James about her homework and so she missed break time altogether. She ate her lunch as quickly as she could and ran out to look for Ben.

'I'm behind the big tree,' she thought to herself, hoping that Ben could still read her thoughts.

Sure enough, he bounded up. "You can't go round calling Mrs Lopez a mad fish," he laughed.

"I didn't say it. I just thought it."

"I know. Aren't these superpowers cool?"

"It's a nightmare! I can't jump on anything without shooting off like a rubber ball – not to mention you being in my head…"

"But how can you say it's not cool to have superpowers, Ella? You've just got to learn to control them. Look at this!"

He leant on the tree and pinged off towards the school fence. Then he pinged back again at the tree and then hit the fence even harder. This time it broke, leaving Ben sprawled on the pavement outside.

"Ben Reagan! Ella Bryant! What on earth do you think you're doing?" It was Mrs Lopez, hanging out of her office window.

"Is this national vandalism week? Come to my office now!"

It had to go down as the worst school day ever. Ella got a week's detentions after school, a letter to her mum and dad asking for money to repair the toilet and lectures from Mrs Lopez, Mr Grant her form teacher, her mum, her dad and then her mum again after she'd talked to Ben's mum. On top of all that she had double homework to catch up on as well.

When Ella had been younger, she had dreamed of having superpowers. Now she really had them, she just wanted to get rid of them. But how?

That's it for tonight

Sleep well. We'll find out more about Ella and Ben and their superpowers next time, in superpower kids.

wednesday
or whatever day
it happens to be

Ella got all the way to school before she had a chance to find out if she still had her super bouncing power. Standing in a toilet cubicle she tried a little jump. She had to break her fall on the toilet lid, to stop herself going through the ceiling. The headmistress found the damage and demanded an explanation. Ella quickly came up with one and might have got away with it if Ben hadn't insisted on showing off his sideways bouncing powers at lunchtime – flattening a school fence right outside the headmistress's office. Now they were both in big trouble. Ella desperately wanted to get rid of her strange powers and just get back to normal. Now read on...

When Ella got to school the next morning, she went looking for Ben, but no one had seen him. By break time it was clear that he wasn't around and eventually she plucked up the courage to ask one of his mates, Jordan.

"He's in hospital. Broke his shoulder, somehow. Mr Giggs seemed to think he might have fallen out of a tree in his garden, or something. Surprised you didn't know, being his girlfriend and all that."

"I'm not his girlfriend!"

"He always says you are."

"Does he? Well I'm not!" She waited a moment. "Do you know which hospital he's in?"

"The General I guess. We could go and visit together."

"No! Thanks. I'll probably go with my mum. Bye."

Ella turned and ran for cover over in the skipping corner. Why was Ben saying she was his girlfriend?

"Come on Ella, you hold for a while," Heather shouted.

In a bit of a daze, Ella took the rope, mindlessly singing the rhyme as she thought about Ben.

"Come on Ella, swap!" Jessica took the rope and pushed her into the middle. Ella jumped in alongside Lilly. It was fine. No crazy bouncing. Then Lilly went to skipping with two feet.

"Come on, Ella, get in step."

Ella tried one jump and felt the spring. Why had she thought it might have gone? She tried landing on one leg, but she was off balance and crashed into Lilly, bringing them both down on the hard playground.

Ella was grateful for the bleeding knee – it was a good excuse to leave the skipping. Lilly too had a bad graze and both of them limped off to see Mrs Dolby in the school office.

"We'll be OK for PE, won't we miss?" Lilly asked Mrs Dolby anxiously.

"Yes. It should be fine. You like the vaulting horse, don't you Lilly?"

The vaulting horse! Ella couldn't go and

jump over the vaulting horse. One leap and she'd end up on the school roof!

"I can't bend my knee, miss," she whimpered.

"Nonsense Ella. It's just a little graze. A bit of movement will do it good. Now off you go."

They had an hour of English before PE. Ella kept quiet and worked hard. When the bell went for afternoon break, she grabbed hold of Lilly.

"If anyone asks, just say I hurt my knee and had to go home."

Without giving Lilly a chance to say anything, Ella grabbed her coat and walked out of the school gate, all the time dreading the shout from a teacher. As soon as she hit the street she started to run.

It didn't take long to get to the hospital. A kindly nurse showed her to Ben's ward. He was on his own, asleep.

"Ben, it's me."

He opened his eyes.

"What happened?" she asked.

"Pinged too hard," he muttered. "Can't control it. I feel like a rubber band."

"Ben? Have you told anyone?"

"Do you think I'm mad? Do you think they'd believe me? And if I show them, what are they going to do? Lock me up somewhere probably!"

"What shall we do then?"

"Have you still got the sweet wrapper?"

Ella felt in her pocket. It was still there.

"Go back to the park. See if there's another one. See if anyone recognises it."

"What if there isn't? What if someone doesn't?"

"I don't know. Ella? Are you supposed
to be here?"

"No, I'm bunking off PE."

"Well you'd better get out of here because
I can see my mum coming."

Ella darted behind the curtain next to the
bed just in time. When she thought Ben's
mum looked busy, she dived under the
next bed and made a quick exit, dreading
a shout from a grown-up for the second
time that day.

When she got back to school, she just
had time to slip through the broken fence
(thanks Ben) and around the side of the

school to join her
classmates as they
came out. She
could see Lilly
trying to get near
her through the
throng, but Ella
kept out of the way.

"Can we go to the park mum?"
she asked before either of her
sisters could come up with
another idea.

When they got to
the park,
Ella said
she was just
going to ask some of the skateboarders
about Ben. She went over to the bench,
took the wrapper out of her pocket and
casually wafted it around hoping that
someone might say something. It didn't
work. Her mother looked at her strangely
from the other side of the playground so
she got up and ambled over to the
skateboarders. Jordan was there!

"Ella! Cool. Came to see some moves, huh?"

"I'm just here with my mum and sisters."

"Yeah, right!" he laughed and pushed off
on his board.

'I don't even like you!' she thought to herself. If only they hadn't eaten the sweet! Why hadn't she just left it here on the bench? Why did she have to go and eat it? How was she ever going to get rid of these powers? All they seemed to do was get her into trouble and make her lie all the time.

"Perhaps I can help," a high voice said from somewhere behind a bush.

She hadn't been speaking out loud! She looked around.

"I'm over here," the voice said.

Peering low under a big green bush she made eye contact with something. What was it?

"I'm Shambo," it said.

"What's a Shambo?" Ella asked.

"I think I'm what you people call an alien. Someone from another planet? And the reason I can hear your thoughts is that you are speaking my language in your head. We don't speak out loud. We think talk. But you can't hear my thoughts, can you?"

"No. I don't understand."

"That wrapper you have."

"The sweet?" She took it from her pocket.

"It's not a sweet. It's my re-entry pill."

Ella stumbled backwards and sat down on the bench.

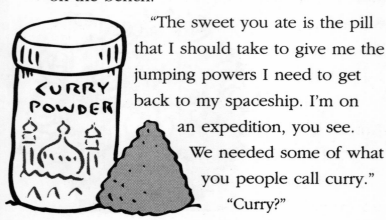

"The sweet you ate is the pill that I should take to give me the jumping powers I need to get back to my spaceship. I'm on an expedition, you see. We needed some of what you people call curry."

"Curry?"

"Well not curry exactly, but some of the hot spices that make curry. They make our spacecraft move very fast, but yours is only one of eight planets that have it. And yours is the only one that doesn't know it makes the best fuel for spacecraft, so it's easy to borrow it here."

"Do you mean steal it?"

"My use of your language is not always so good. But here in your city there are many restaurants that have much spice. We don't need so much; a little from each one. Nobody misses it, but it means that we will be able to outrun the Dingfor tribes on our way home. Very important to outrun the Dingfor…"

Ella butted in.

"Look I'm very pleased you like Chicken Korma, but…"

"What is Chicken Korma?"

"Never mind. All I want to know is how do we get rid of these powers. I mean is there a pill that puts everything back to normal?"

"Oh yes."

"Brilliant. So can me and Ben have one please?"

"Ben?" the Shambo asked.

"He's my friend.

We ate half of your pill each. He now pings from side to side and can hear everything I think. I now ping up and down and apparently think in a language from another planet. We both want to get back to normal please!"

"I don't think that will be possible."

"But the pill that changes everything back?"

"I ate that when I arrived to stop myself pinging all over the place on your planet. You have such thin air you see and we are so light."

"But there's another one, right?"

"Oh yes. These pills are not scarce. We have many pills. I can take one that will allow me to hover like one of your funny helicopters and another that helps me to speak Farg, an interesting language..."

"Shambo! Where do we get another normal pill?"

"From my ship."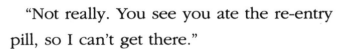

"Great."

"Not really. You see you ate the re-entry pill, so I can't get there."

"But they'll send someone down soon to look for you."

"I am not sure that I am that popular."

Now her mum was coming over.

Ella switched to think-talking. 'What can we do?'

"There is only one thing. You have the jumping power. You can go."

'No way!' Ella thought as her mother sat beside her on the bench. 'Way too scary.

We'll wait for you to be rescued.'

"Could be a long wait," the Shambo whispered as her mum sat down.

"What did you say love? Are you alright? One minute, you seem distant. Like you're on another planet. The next minute, you're all jumpy."

Ella tried to ignore the high-pitched chortling from the bush behind and cuddled up to her mum.

'I'll think about it Shambo,' she thought. 'Now shut up or we'll both end up in a circus.'

That's it for tonight

Sleep well. We'll find out more about Ella and Ben and their superpowers next time, in superpower kids.

thursday

or whatever day
it happens to be

When Ben's bouncing antics landed him in hospital, Ella decided to go back to the park and see if she could find out who the sweet had belonged to. Sitting on the bench where it had all begun, wishing they had never eaten it, she was amazed to hear a squeaky voice explain that it wasn't a sweet – it was a re-entry pill. The voice belonged to someone or something called 'Shambo'. He explained that he was visiting our planet, but couldn't get back to his spaceship because by eating the pill, Ella and Ben had got the jumping powers he needed to return. The only way for Ella and Ben to get back to normal and for Shambo to get back home was for Ella to use her new powers to fly up to his spaceship. But is she brave enough? Now read on...

If Ella had thought that Tuesday had been her worst ever day at school, Thursday certainly didn't begin any better.

When they arrived at the school gates, Mrs Lopez was waiting.

"Mrs Bryant. Do you think that you and Ella could both step into my office?" the headmistress asked her mum in a very serious tone.

It was serious. Not only had her PE teacher noted her absence, but Mrs Lopez

had actually seen her sneaking back
through the broken fence. To cap it all,
when they had been in the park, Ella was
supposed to have been in detention –
with Mrs Lopez.

Ella stumbled through a series of
half-excuses and vague stammered replies
to their questions, hoping to put them off.
The adults were both angry and concerned.

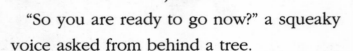

Back in class, she found people treating her differently. Lilly and Heather seemed a bit off-ish. Melinda, the hardest girl in the class, wanted to hang out with her. Life was upside down. She tried to keep herself to herself.

At lunchtime she found a quiet place on her own, well away from Mrs Lopez's office, and thought hard for Shambo to join her.

"So you are ready to go now?" a squeaky voice asked from behind a tree.

"No! Not now! I don't want to get in any more trouble. Tonight. After bedtime."

"OK, I will come to your house."

"Shambo. One last thing. I need to see you, so I know what to expect."

"OK, but it won't help you. I took a pill so I would look like animals that live on your planet."

There was a rustling in the leaves and
out of the grass came a little brown mouse.
The strange thing was that it was walking
on its hind legs.

"Shambo! You're lucky you didn't get
killed, going into kitchens looking like that!"

"It is true, my spice collecting was not
without incident. Let me tell you." He leant
against the trunk of the tree
and talked solidly for
fifteen minutes.
Ella didn't mind.
She didn't want to
talk to anyone else.
She felt like an
outsider. An alien.

"Of course you are half alien really,"
Shambo said unhelpfully.

The bell went. "Come to my flat at nine,"
she said, carefully explaining how to
get there, before going to keep her
appointment with the school counsellor.

Ella heard her dad come in to check on her, but pretended to be asleep and he went to the lounge. Now was her chance. She opened the bedroom window and Shambo was there.

"I can't go," she said before he had time to make some long-winded speech.

"You must."

"My mum and dad are going to freak out if they find I'm out of bed. And they're bound to check again. They're really worried about me."

"This is not the problem. Our time is different from yours. You may feel that you are on our spaceship for a long time, but actually it will only be minutes here."

"But there's another problem?"

"Perhaps. A small one."

"Tell me."

"You ate half the pill. You have the up-power. But Ben has the sideways power. If the ship has moved, it may be difficult for you to land on it."

"That settles it. I'm not going."

"Then you are sure to be able to enjoy
many more school counselling sessions like
you did today."

"You heard that did you?"

"Heard it! You've been complaining about
it in your head all afternoon. It nearly made
me take my eye off a cat. And that's
another reason why you must go. I will not
be able to survive much
longer in this furry outfit
and I have no other pills
here to change my
appearance. If I was
back home, I could..."

"OK. OK. I'll go."
Ella climbed out of the
window, careful not
to land on two feet
as she dropped down
into the little garden.

"Right. Go on then."

"But what do I do?"

"It's simple. All you do is jump from the climbing frame onto the path. You'll shoot up in the air, land again and bounce even higher. Two or three bounces should do it. The magnetic power will then click in and take you to the ship. If the ship is still there."

"What do you mean, if it's still there?"

"I am not the most popular crew member. They may have left without me."

"And if they have?"

"You will have to bounce across to a large lake – or the sea, like your amateur little spacecraft do when they land."

"We're fifty miles from the sea!"

"Don't worry, it will take just a few bounces."

Ella got up on the climbing frame. She was scared, but she couldn't go on being in trouble all her life and Ben was already in hospital. She didn't really have a choice.

"Very wise," Shambo said.

The thought that a mouse that couldn't stop talking would follow her around for the rest of her life listening to her thoughts was the final straw. She jumped before he had a chance to say anything else.

She shot up at such a speed it made her eyes water. The down trip made her ears

pop like they do on an aeroplane. When her feet hit the ground she didn't feel a bump, just a soft but powerful spring as if she were on a huge bouncy castle. The second bounce took her past the windows of the two flats above theirs, so she could see the roof of their building. The third bounce took her above the clouds themselves, the whole of the night sky above her, laid out like a twinkly blanket. As she began to fall back down to earth, she felt herself dragged sideways into a cloud. Instead of dropping back down, her feet rested on something in the mist. Then she felt her head being pressed down until she was bent over, as if she were trying to stand up on her sister's bottom bunk.

Slowly the mist cleared. Now she could see she was in a smooth, spherical, silver spaceship, like a dome tent. Everything was tiny. Including the little worm-like creatures that were looking at her curiously with their

large, beady pink eyes. One of them put
a sweet or pill in its mouth.

"Pwwwwweeeeeeeeeeeee Fwaaaaar,"
it said.

Ella was horrified. If they couldn't talk
her language, she was going to be in
big trouble.

The worm took another pill. "Sorry.
Wrong language pill. Very confusing.
So many planets. How did you get here
please?"

Ella took a deep breath. How could she
explain about the pill and Ben and her new

powers and Shambo and everything that had happened to her?

"I see," said the worm-like creature. All the others nodded. "It is good you can talk our language. It's a shame you cannot understand it. Never mind. You will do. We must go."

Ella crouched down to get more comfortable. "What do you mean, go?"

"We have been waiting too long for Shambo. Now you explain. We will go."

"No, you can't! I must go back with his re-entry pill and you must give me a pill so that me and Ben can live normally again."

All the worm-like creatures looked at one another in a circle and Ella realised they had eyes in the front and back of their heads.

"This is not possible."

Ella thought frantically, aware that they were listening to it all going round in her head. What had Shambo said about the spice? Oh, yes. They needed it to fuel the spaceship to out-run the Dingos or something like that.

The talking worm cut across her thoughts, "I think you mean the Dingfor tribes of Scelarian Four. You are right – it is dangerous without spice-speed. But perhaps it is more dangerous allowing you to go back to your planet, knowing what the spice can do. There are enough creatures flying up here without humans joining in."

"I won't tell anyone."

The worms put themselves in a circle again, presumably discussing what to do. It was awful for Ella. She knew that they could hear every thought she had, while she couldn't hear anything they said, unless they decided to eat a pill and talk in her language. She didn't even know anyone's name and there wasn't enough room to sit down. She just wanted her mum.

The worms all moved over, making room for her.

"I am sorry. We have been rude. My name is Veenam. We understand about your mother. We too miss our mother."

"You all have the same mother?"

"Yes, we are brothers and sisters."

"Then how can you possibly think of leaving Shambo down there?"

"We are traders. We spend many hours cooped up in our spaceship. Shambo is difficult."

"Because he never stops talking?"

Veenam turned to one of the other worms for another silent chat.

"You are clever. And you are tall. You

have long arms and big hands. You can carry many pills. You are perhaps more useful than Shambo. We will keep you."

"But he's your brother. Doesn't that mean anything to any of you?"

He shrugged in a wormy way.

"We must sleep now. Then we must go," he said.

Ella watched as they all lay on their backs, their little arms pivoting at the elbows and swinging round and round above their heads like helicopter blades.

This was no life for a nearly ten year old.
She should be running in the park, or
skipping with the girls. What could she do?
She had to think while they were all asleep.

That's it for tonight

Sleep well. We'll find out more about Ella and Ben and their superpowers, in the final part of superpower kids, next time.

friday
or whatever day
it happens to be

What happened last time?

After another terrible day at school during which Ella found herself in the headmistress's office again, she agreed that she would use her jumping powers to go to Shambo's spaceship and get the pills that would make Ben and her normal again. Jumping from the climbing frame, Ella bounced ever higher until suddenly, she found herself inside the ship with about twenty worm-like creatures. But instead of giving her the pills she needed, they decided that she would be more useful than Shambo – and quieter.
They would rather keep her and leave Shambo on earth. The worms all then went to sleep leaving Ella one last chance to work out how to escape. Now read the final part of "superpower kids"...

Ella knew that she had to think of a good reason why they should swap her for Shambo. If not, she was going to be stuck in an undersized silver dome tent with only worms for company. Ben was going to be in and out of hospital and Shambo was going to end up as cat food.

The arms of the smallest worm nearest to her suddenly stopped going round and it slid over to the side of the ship. A huge compartment suddenly opened up, full of pills. The worm carefully chose one and turned to Ella.

"What is cat food?" it asked.

"I thought you were all asleep," Ella said.

"Not me. I am too sad. Shambo is my best brother. I do not want to leave without him. Please, is it a good thing for Shambo to be cat food?"

Ella explained that it was not a good thing. She imagined her own cat, Dillon, standing at the window with Shambo in his jaws.

The little worm began to shake.
"Please turn the pictures off!"

It's difficult to stop thinking of something
when someone asks you to, but she could
see it was upsetting the little worm and he
or she seemed nice, so Ella imagined
herself at home asleep in her bed – where
she should be.

"Your air coolers
are not working?"
the little worm said.

"My what?"

"You cannot sleep
without air coolers."

It nodded towards the other worms with
their arms going round. Suddenly Ella
realised their arms were acting like fans,
cooling them while they slept.

"What's your name?" Ella asked. She really
wanted to know if it was a boy or a girl
too, but didn't want to sound rude.

"My name is Pling. I am a girl. This is not

rude to wonder," Pling said.

"Do your brothers and sisters really not like Shambo because he talks too much?" Ella asked.

"Yes. We cannot sleep very long because our arms get tired and then we get hot and wake up. Shambo keeps everyone awake with his talking. They get cross and it makes for a very difficult trip. The older ones think they will go mad by the time we get home, so they are pleased he is missing."

"Even though you haven't got the spice you need?"

"They think they would rather run the risk of the Dingfors than have to put up with Shambo!" Pling looked really miserable now.

Ella looked at all the pills. Why couldn't they give Shambo a pill to stop him talking so much?

"Because it is not allowed," the little worm answered, reading her thoughts. "We can only change ourselves outside the ship for a mission. It is the law."

Ella had another thought. What if they didn't need their arms to cool themselves?

"But we do. If we do not have a breeze, we cannot sleep."

Ella thought about the fan on her bedside table. Pling didn't react. She then imagined it turned on, blowing air across her as she slept. The little worm nodded, then frowned again.

"This could solve half the problem. If they could sleep longer they would be less cross with Shambo. You are clever. This would work."

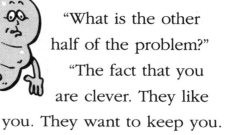

"What is the other half of the problem?"

"The fact that you are clever. They like you. They want to keep you. They have made up their minds."

"And you?"

"I too like you, but I still want my best brother back. I am sorry to say this. I do not want to be rude either."

Ella patted Pling's head. It was hot and dry. "I like you too, but I want to go home. If I can solve the other half of the problem, will you be able to give me the non-bouncing pills we need and a new re-entry pill for Shambo?"

"Oh yes. If the old ones allow it."

Now she knew what she had to do. She just had to think!

In her head she imagined herself in a huge football stadium, with a stage and a microphone. Taking a great big imaginary

breath she shouted into the microphone.

'**ITS NOT FAIR ON SHAMBO!**'

Every single one of the worms shot
upright in fright.

Now she knew how to get their attention!

Using the imaginary mike, she carried on.

'**IF YOU DO NOT SWAP ME WITH SHAMBO I
WILL THINK AS LOUD AS THIS FOR THE WHOLE
TIME I AM ON THIS SHIP.**'

The worms were huddling around the
outside walls. It was working.

'IT WILL DRIVE YOU MAD. YOU WILL SLEEP LESS THAN YOU DO WHEN SHAMBO IS HERE!'

Veenam came forward as if struggling against a huge wind.

"It will not work," he said. "We will just give you a pill to keep you quiet."

'YOU ARE NOT ALLOWED TO GIVE ME A PILL WHILE I'M ON THE SHIP,' she shouted into her microphone, pleased that Pling had told her this. All the worms now stared at the little one.

In her mind, she now turned off the microphone.

'If you allow me to go back, Shambo will bring something that will solve your sleeping problem,' she thought quietly. Now she pictured her bedroom with the fan. Like an advert on television, she then zoomed in on the fan, feeling the breeze blowing her hair. Then she imagined it in the spaceship blowing gently over all the worms as they lay sleeping, arms resting comfortably by their sides.

The worms were now in a circle, obviously talking. Then Ella noticed that Pling looked worried, as if the argument were going in the wrong way.

Ella grabbed the imaginary microphone again and bellowed into it.

'IT"S UP TO YOU. BUT DON"T FORGET WHAT LIFE WILL BE LIKE WITH ME ON BOARD!'

Veenam held up his little hands. "OK. OK," he said, "I will give you the pills you need. But if Shambo returns without the cooling thing he will be sent straight back, looking exactly like you. This will not be easy for you to live with."

Ella thought for a moment what home would be like with a new identical chattering twin. All the worms nodded knowingly.

'**DEAL**,' she thought-shouted through her imaginary microphone, just to wipe the smug looks off their faces.

Suddenly the dome became a mass of opening doors and all the worms were busy. Pling gave her three pills. One she recognised immediately.

"You are right. This green one is Shambo's re-entry pill. Your landing pill is blue – the same colour as your sea where your spaceships land – and the purple one will return you and your friend back to normal."

Ella gave him a little hug, nodded at the other worms and gratefully made for the door. The second she stepped through it, she was falling. But which was the landing pill? Purple, blue or green?

It wasn't until she saw the moonlight on

the sea that she remembered. Blue is for landing. She swallowed the blue pill, just as her town and her park came into view. Closer now, her street, her flats, the garden, still at a frightening speed.

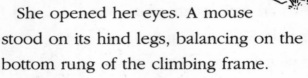

Ella shut her eyes.

"Did you get them?"

She opened her eyes. A mouse stood on its hind legs, balancing on the bottom rung of the climbing frame.

"Shambo?"

"No, I'm some other talking mouse! Of course it's me. Now give me the re-entry pill and let me get out of here, before they leave without me!"

"Here's your pill. But I have to get you something else to take back."

Ella crept into her room and grabbed the fan. When she got back to the garden, instead of Shambo she found her cat,

Dillon, sitting on the patio licking his paws.

"Dillon, you've ruined everything!"
she hissed at him, tears welling up.

"What's he done?" a girl's voice asked.

Ella looked up, to see herself! Or at least
a 'mousey' version of herself.

"It's me, Shambo," he said. "My re-entry
pill changed me into you. So I can carry
that," he said pointing to the fan.

"It would have been a bit
heavy for Shambo
the mouse."

Ella laughed. "I think it was just to remind me to give it to you. Good luck Shambo."

He nodded. "Ella? Next time you find a sweet in the park..."

"I'll leave it well alone," she called, as Shambo shot upwards into the night sky.

Just one more thing to do, she thought, holding the last sweet in her hand.

It was easy to persuade her mum to go and visit Ben after detention the next day, but it was much more difficult to get him on his own. While the mums fussed around, Ella sat quietly next to his bed, remembering the whole adventure for Ben. He looked as if he might burst with excitement as he read her mind. When the mums finally went to buy tea, Ben practically shouted:

"Wow, Ella. Space and everything! Let's not take the pill. Hold on to me and we can go together. It'll be wicked."

But Ella already had the wrapper off.

She bit half of it and leant sideways against
the bed. It felt springy! She tapped lightly
on the floor and felt the familiar ping.
She had the wrong half!

Quickly, she grabbed Ben by his pyjamas
took the wet half out of her mouth and
pushed it into his with her fingers. He
looked as if he might spit it out, so she
held her hand over his mouth.

"Ella. What are you doing?" Ben's mum shouted from across the ward.

Ella slid off the bed and put the other half of the sweet in her mouth.

"He was going to bounce out of bed," Ella said.

Ben swallowed hard. "I'll never eat mashed potato again," he said wincing.

"'Bouncing? Mashed potato?" his mum asked, really confused now. "'Are you OK?"

Ella backed away as Ben's mum started fussing. She tried a little jump.

Nothing.

That was definitely OK with her.

That's it!
Sleep well.

Then what happened?

If you want to know what happened to Shambo when he got back to his spaceship, look up m2fbooks.com on the Internet and use this special password in the password area: SUPERPOWERS

Have you read any of the other monday 2 friday books?

the good pirate

When Denise Grate asks to look under Pirate Pete's eye-patch – and sees he really doesn't have an eye – Fergus knows his eighth birthday is going to be talked about forever. But as the pirate ship sails with Fergus trapped on board, he finds out there's a lot more to pirating than parties. Follow Fergus's adventure over five nights in the good pirate.

More fab stories to look out for:

**The Summer Spirit
The School Trip**

Find out more at **m2fbooks.com**

m2f